Poppleton
EVERY DAY

Read more
Poppleton
books!

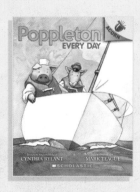

Poppleton
EVERY DAY

Written by Newbery Medalist
CYNTHIA RYLANT

Illustrated by
MARK TEAGUE

ACORN™
SCHOLASTIC INC.

Library of Congress Cataloging-in-Publication Data

Names: Rylant, Cynthia, author. | Teague, Mark, illustrator. | Rylant, Cynthia. Poppleton ; 3.
Title: Poppleton every day / written by Newbery Medalist Cynthia Rylant ; illustrated by Mark Teague. Description: [New edition] | New York : Acorn/Scholastic Inc., [2020] | Series: Poppleton ; 3 | Originally published: New York : Blue Sky Press, 1998. | Summary: Poppleton the pig goes stargazing, tries out a new bed before he buys it, and goes sailing for the first time.
Identifiers: LCCN 2018055969| ISBN 9781338566710 (pb) | ISBN 9781338566727 (hc) | ISBN 9781338566819 (ebk)
Subjects: LCSH: Poppleton (Fictitious character) — Juvenile fiction. | Swine — Juvenile fiction. | Friendship — Juvenile fiction. | Stars — Juvenile fiction. | Sailing — Juvenile fiction. | Beds — Juvenile fiction. | CYAC: Pigs — Fiction. | Stars — Fiction. | Beds — Fiction. | Sailing — Fiction.
Classification: LCC PZ7.R982 Pv 2020 | DDC 813.54 [E] — dc23
LC record available at https://lccn.loc.gov/2018055969

10 9 8 7 6 5 4 3 2 1   20 21 22 23 24

Printed in China   62
This edition first printing, January 2020
Book design by Maria Mercado

CONTENTS

MEET THE CHARACTERS

Poppleton

Fillmore

Hudson

THE SKY

Poppleton's friend Hudson was
visiting one night.

"Let's go look at the sky,"
said Hudson.

Poppleton got blankets,
and they went to look at the sky.

"I see the Big Dipper," said Hudson.

"Yes," said Poppleton.

"I see the Little Dipper," said Hudson.

"Yes," said Poppleton.

"I even see Venus!" said Hudson.
"Do you see Venus, Poppleton?"

But Poppleton did not answer.
He had his eyes closed.

"What's wrong, Poppleton?" asked Hudson.
"Are you sick?"

"I am dizzy," said Poppleton.
"Stars make me dizzy."

"Oh dear," said Hudson.

"The sky is so big and deep," said Poppleton.
"I get seasick."

"Oh my," said Hudson.

"I wish I could look," said Poppleton.
"But I can't."

"How sad," said Hudson.
"Let me think."

While Poppleton closed his eyes,
Hudson thought.

"I have an idea," said Hudson.

He cut a tiny hole in his blanket
and put it over Poppleton's head.

"Now you'll see only a tiny sky,"
said Hudson.

Poppleton peeped up at two little stars.

"Beautiful!" said Poppleton.

And the two friends stargazed
all night long.

THE NEW BED

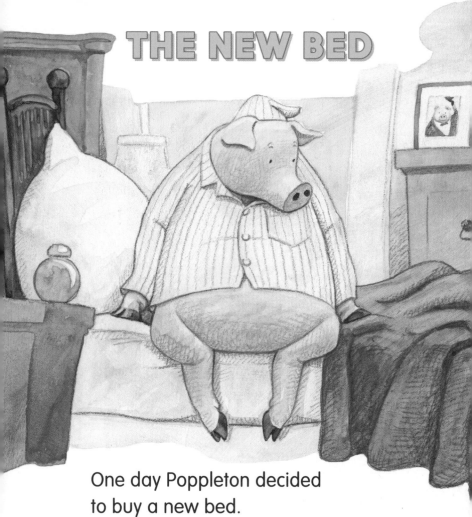

One day Poppleton decided
to buy a new bed.
He liked his old bed.
But he'd had it since he was a boy.
Now he wanted a grown-up bed.

So Poppleton went to the bed store.

"Do you have a bed just right for a pig?"
he asked the saleslady.

"Hmmm," she said, looking Poppleton over.
"Right this way."

Poppleton followed the saleslady
to the biggest bed in the store.

It was vast!
It was enormous!

"It's just my size!" said Poppleton.

He climbed on to test the bed.

He lay on his back.

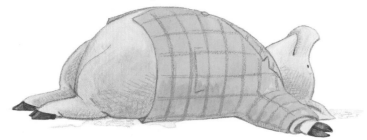

He lay on his side.

He lay with one leg over the edge.

He lay with both legs over the edge.

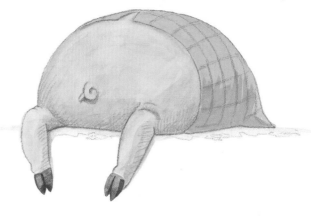

He lay on his head with
his bottom in the air.

"How many different ways do you sleep?"
asked the saleslady.

"About twenty," said Poppleton.

"Do you have any books?" he asked.

The saleslady brought Poppleton a book.

Poppleton propped up some pillows
and read a few pages.

The saleslady looked at her watch.
"Do you want to buy the bed?"
she asked Poppleton.

"I don't know yet," said Poppleton.
"Do you have any crackers?"

The saleslady brought Poppleton
some crackers.
He got crumbs everywhere.

"Do you want the bed?"
asked the saleslady.

"I don't know yet," said Poppleton.
"Do you have a TV?"

The saleslady brought Poppleton a TV.
He watched a game show.

The saleslady checked her watch.
"Do you want the bed?"
she asked Poppleton.

"I don't know yet," said Poppleton.
"I have to check one more thing.
Do you have any bluebirds?"

"Pardon me?" said the saleslady.

"I always wake up to bluebirds,"
said Poppleton.
"Do you have any?"

The saleslady went outside
and got three bluebirds to come in
and sing to Poppleton.

Poppleton lay with his eyes closed
and a big smile on his face.

"**Now** do you want the bed?"
asked the saleslady.

"Certainly!" said Poppleton.

And he picked up the book, the crackers,
the bluebirds, and the bed,
and happily went home.

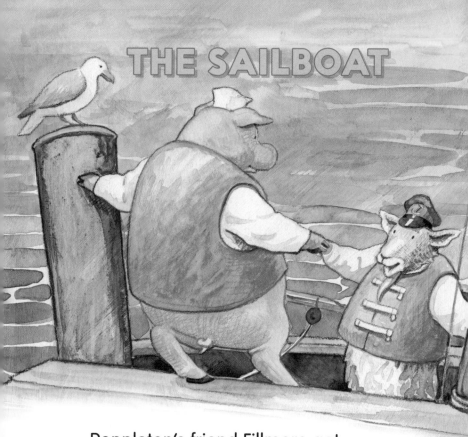

Poppleton's friend Fillmore got
a new sailboat.

"Will you come sailing?" asked Fillmore.

"Sure!" said Poppleton.
So he went in Fillmore's boat.

Poppleton had never been sailing.
He didn't know what to do.

"Do you know what to do, Fillmore?"
asked Poppleton.

"Sure," said Fillmore.
"Just sit back and relax."

Poppleton sat back.

Suddenly the boat leaned to the far, far left.

"I am not relaxed, Fillmore!"
cried Poppleton.

The boat leaned to the far, far right.

"NOT RELAXED!" Poppleton cried.

"Relax!" said Fillmore.

Then the boat caught a strong wind.
It bounced up and down, up and down
on the waves.

"I AM NOT RELAXED!" cried Poppleton.

A big storm came.

"NOT RELAXED!" Poppleton cried.

Then the sailboat flipped over.

"DEFINITELY NOT RELAXED!" cried Poppleton, swimming beside Fillmore.

"Relax!" said Fillmore.

Poppleton and Fillmore climbed back
into the boat.

They sailed back to shore.

"Wasn't that fun?" asked Fillmore.

"Well, not all of it," said Poppleton.

"The leaning was fun,
and the bouncing was fun,
and the flipping over was fun,"
said Fillmore.

"Yes, but the shark wasn't,"
said Poppleton.

"SHARK!!!???" shouted Fillmore,
and he went screaming down the road.

"Gee, Fillmore," called Poppleton.
"RELAX!"

Then Poppleton went home, smiling,
and did just that.

ABOUT THE CREATORS

CYNTHIA RYLANT

has written more than one hundred books, including *Dog Heaven*, *Cat Heaven*, and the Newbery Medal–winning novel *Missing May*. She lives with her pets in Oregon.

MARK TEAGUE

lives in New York State with his family, which includes a dog and two cats, but no pigs, llamas, or goats, and only an occasional mouse. Mark is the author of many books and the illustrator of many more, including the How Do Dinosaurs series.

YOU CAN DRAW

1. Draw an oval. (Sketch lightly so you can erase as you go!)

2. Add arms and legs.

3. Circles make his head and ears. Add two triangle horns.

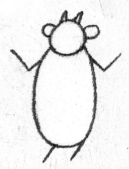

4. Draw Fillmore's face. Don't forget his billy goat beard!

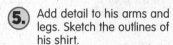

5. Add detail to his arms and legs. Sketch the outlines of his shirt.

6. Add more details to his shirt and legs. Add his hooves, too.

7. Fill in details such as buttons, fur, and eyebrows.

8. Color in your drawing!

Poppleton and Fillmore go sailing together.
Imagine **you** and Fillmore go sailing.
What would your boat look like?
Where would it take you?
Write and draw your story!

scholastic.com/acorn